**BUILD
UNIVERSES**

THE ADVENTURES OF JAMES BONE, SECRET AGENT

JAMES BONE
AND THE ITALIAN JOB
BY FRANK BELL

europe books

© 2021 **Europe Books** | London
www.europebooks.co.uk – info@europebooks.co.uk

ISBN 979-12-201-1417-2
First edition: October 2021

Distribution for the United Kingdom: **Vine House Distribution ltd**

Printed for Italy by Rotomail Italia
Finito di stampare nel mese di ottobre 2021
presso Rotomail Italia S.p.A. - Vignate (MI)

James Bone and the Italian Job

DEDICATION

Finally, and at last my darlin' Gail. I have written this story and published this book especially for you xxx and I do hope that many other readers will enjoy reading the first adventure of James Bone Secret Agent.

INTRODUCTION

"Let me start by introducing myself. I am a very British bulldog and my name is 'Winston'. My master chose my name in honour of the famous British Prime Minister, Winston Churchill.

There aren't many bulldogs who can boast that they live next door to someone very important, but I jolly well can. I live with my master, the Chancellor of the Exchequer, at No. 11 Downing Street, and just a few strides down the pavement at No. 10 lives the Prime Minister of Great Britain. I've lived at No. 11 for as long as I can remember, which is 14 of your human years which, if my math is correct, makes me aged 98 in doggie years. Recently, it dawned on me just how old I was getting, so I decided it was high time I put pen to paper to write about all the wonderful friends I have made here and the exciting adventures we have shared together. So, with no further ado, I invite you to sit back and enjoy the adventures of two of my very special friends, secret agent James Bone and Humphrey, the Downing Street cat."

CHAPTER ONE - A PERFECT DAY

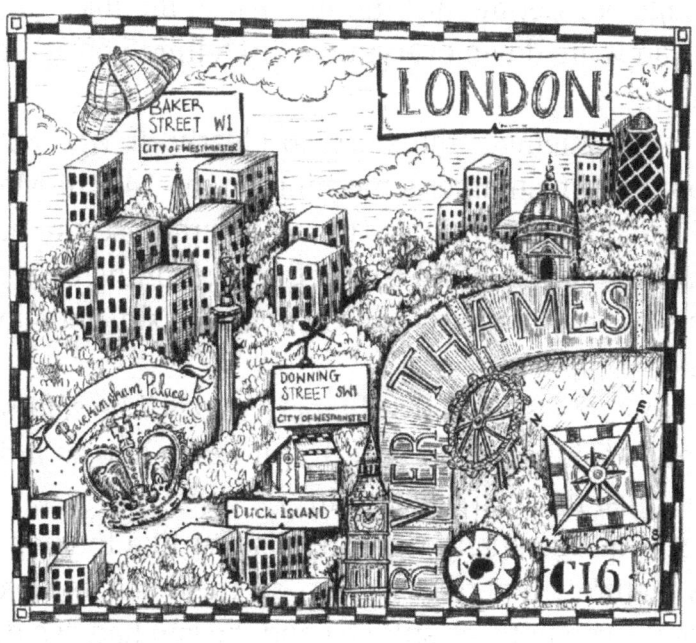

"I just have to say... Downing Street is a really marvellous place to live. It's always busy and there's always something happening, or just about to happen. Lots of people rush backwards and forward visiting the Prime Minister and my master, the Chancellor of the Exchequer. Why, it seems like only yesterday that my next-door neighbour

Humphrey the Downing Street cat, told me the exciting tale about the time his best friend, the famous secret agent James Bone, asked for his help on a top-secret mission to rescue the Queen of England. Let me just dip my pen in the inkwell so I can write down everything I'm telling you as I go along.

I can remember the story so clearly. It was early on a warm summer's morning on the 14th of May. The sun shone brightly out of a turquoise sky and not a breath of wind stirred the air. Rolling over on his back, Humphrey looked up at the sky and gave a deep sigh.

"Now this is what I call a perfect day," he said out loud. "The sky's so beautiful it looks like an artist has just finished painting it."

He was absolutely right. It was just like looking at a picture – a perfect picture, so fresh and so clean, as if the paint was still wet and the sun had decided to come out just to dry it. The only thing that made Humphrey realise, he was not looking at a picture was the muffled roar of a distant plane and the fast-disappearing trail of white vapour it left behind, as it swiftly cut across the clear blue sky.

A loud series of clicking sounds woke Humphrey from his daydream and brought him back to reality. He rolled over onto his chest and peered over the edge of the windowsill to see what all the fuss was about. Far beneath, on the street below, the Prime Minister's car had just pulled up outside the front door of No. 10.

"I see" he said to himself. "The boss is back." The clicking sound was the noise of the cameras firing off, as the waiting pack of journalists pushed forward, the noise of their cameras louder and faster than a field full of crickets on a summer's evening.

"Time to pop down and make the PM welcome," thought Humphrey. "He does seem to like it when I jump up into his lap and let him stroke me. I think it helps the old boy relax and de-stresses him a little." Humphrey arched his back, then stretched out for all he was worth, before he strolled off the windowsill and in through the open window. He jumped onto the bed, then down onto the thick, rich carpet. Casually, he took a look around before strolling lazily through the open bedroom doors, then out onto the landing. After another casual glance, he strolled gently along to the wide staircase, which would lead him downstairs to the PM's study.

Humphrey peered keenly around the study door and spotted the PM, gently rocking backwards and forwards in his favourite chair. His eyes were closed, his shoes were off, and his feet were comfortably crossed on top of his desk. With one easy leap, Humphrey landed softly on the PM's lap. The PM briefly opened his eyes, then began to lazily stroke the back of Humphrey's neck; the cat's response was to elegantly curl himself in a circle, close his eyes and purr deeply.

"Humphrey, you sound as loud as a motorbike engine," said the PM in a sleepy voice. A few moments later, when the PM's secretary popped his head around the door, they were both fast asleep; one purring loudly, the other gently snoring. Suddenly, without any warning, the quiet of their afternoon nap was shattered by the loud ringing of the PM's emergency telephone. The PM shot out of his chair. As he jumped up, he spilled Humphrey out of his lap and down towards the floor. Humphrey was already wide awake and executed a perfect back flip before landing safely on the floor. That just goes to prove the old saying, 'cats always land on their feet', thought Humphrey, as he settled down to watch a very flustered PM take the phone call.

"Yes… yes… yes… I understand completely," said the PM, nodding his head furiously as he spoke. Then, for a second or two, he held the phone away from his ear, covered the mouthpiece, and yelled in the general direction of his office door.

"Get me the heads of MI6 and MI5 on the line immediately… *if not sooner!*" he added loudly, in an effort to hurry people along. Slamming the phone down into its cradle, he let out a huge sigh before easing himself back down into his chair. He paused for a second, then glanced over at a very calm-looking Humphrey.

"It's all right for you Humph old boy; you're so lucky you're a cat and don't know what's happening. But I must say, it's a pity you can't understand what I'm saying, as I have a huge problem on my hands and right now, I could use all the help I can get. Late last night, Humphrey… Her Royal Majesty the Queen was kidnapped!"

CHAPTER TWO - DUCK ISLAND

Humphrey looked up at the PM, brushed up against his legs, then trotted off towards the back garden. Humphrey had understood every single word the PM had spoken, and had decided it was time to visit his best friend, secret agent James Bone. He wanted to find out if there was any way James could help find the Queen.

"That's the trouble with humans," he thought, as he made his way out of the door and across the back garden lawn. "They think we are all just dumb animals without any brains; it *really makes me mad*. I do believe old Winston was right when he said, 'If humans had just half of our brainpower, they would be twice as clever as they think they are!'"

Humphrey took his usual route to James Bone's secret home. First, he expertly climbed to the top of the large, sprawling rose tree in the far corner of the garden. From there he made an easy jump to the top of the wall that surrounded No. 10. Next came the tricky bit. Balancing himself carefully, Humphrey coiled up like a spring, took a deep breath and leapt through the air to the ground. He landed beautifully, and with the lightness and grace that only cats and ballet dancers possess.

He quickly ran past the Foreign Office, across Horse Guards Road and into St James's Park. Once in the park, he headed straight for James Bone's home on 'Duck Island'.

James' home was a very spacious, comfortable and modern red-coloured kennel, which had been filled to bursting point with the latest secret gadgets and devices CI6 could supply. The kennel was cleverly disguised and carefully hidden behind a circle of thick, green bushes in the centre of Duck Island. As an agent working for CI6 (Canine Intelligence 6), it was vital that James kept his whereabouts as secret as possible.

Humphrey was very honoured as he was the only

friend James' had shown the secret path that led to his kennel to. As Humphrey trotted happily along the path, he knew James would be lying spreadeagled in his king-size dog box, carefully watching a wall full of plasma screens, which showed every move Humphrey was making. When Humphrey was about 10 metres away from the kennel, he stopped, then carefully stood on a large, square, brass metal plate. He took a moment to make himself comfortable then stood perfectly still.

This was James' Body Recognition Authorisation Scanning System, or B.R.A.S.S. for short. It was a fantastic contraption James had invented with the boffins over at CI6. Like all good ideas the principle was simple. When someone stood on the plate, a powerful beam of light switched on and surrounded it. The beam of light checked the image of whoever was standing on the plate and compared the readings with the details held in its data bank. If the details matched the data bank, the light went out and the visitor could proceed towards the door. But if the details failed to match… Well, let's just say a very powerful laser blaster, capable of destroying a small car, was constantly trained towards the brass plate, and James' paw hovered over the red button until he got the all-clear.

The light went off and Humphrey breathed a sigh of relief before hurrying towards the door of the kennel. On the door was fixed a shiny, silver plaque with the simple inscription: 'Welcome to No. 1 Duck Island'. Before Humphrey could reach the knocker, the door opened and there before him stood his best friend, James Bone.

"Come in, Humphrey old man, I watched your progress all the way along my secret path. I must say, you seemed to be in quite a hurry, so I'm guessing you've got something rather important to tell me."

"I'm surprised you haven't heard already James," replied Humphrey, excitedly. "Your lot over at CI6 are usually on the case pretty fast. I left the PM's office just a few minutes ago. I was listening to him speak with someone on the phone, who was telling him that Her Majesty the Queen has been kidnapped! As soon as I heard the news, I rushed over to tell you. I must say, when I left No. 10, the PM was in a right old state."

James leapt across the room, picked up his special scramble phone and dialled straight through to 'C', the head of CI6 (Canine Intelligence). C's secretary, Miss Sonypennie, an extremely attractive Siamese cat, answered the call.

"Yes James, it's true, the Queen was kidnapped from the palace. C said for you to get over here as fast as you can. Oh, and by the way, James darling,

C is not the only one who wants you over here," she added with a giggle.

"There's no time for that malarkey now, Miss Sonypennie," said James, in a very British and serious voice. "Let's get the Queen safely back in Buck Palace, then maybe you and I can meet up for a few milkshake cocktails. Tell C I'll be with her in five minutes."

"I'll let her know. Oh, and by the way, James, it's a date – just so long as the cocktails are shaken, not stirred." Sonypennie hung up before James had the chance to reply.

James smiled to himself as he put the phone down.

CHAPTER THREE - CI6

"Humphrey, I have to get across to CI6 as quickly as possible. Strap yourself into a seat while I fire up the engines."

Moments later, the room was filled with the roar

of the kennel's engines warming up. Humphrey pressed his paws tightly over his ears to block out the sound. As the kennel slowly lifted off the ground, two short, silver wings automatically slid out from each side of the roof and clicked into place. This was Humphrey's first flight in the kennel; he was so thrilled, he could hardly think straight.

"James!" he yelled excitedly. "Can't people in the park see us taking off?"

"No, Humphrey, old chap. They can hear us, but they can't see us. As we get a little higher off the ground, take a look at the screens on the wall and you will see people looking up in our direction; they are following the sound of the engines, but thankfully they won't see a thing. 'P' at CI6 recently fitted my kennel with a top-secret light-wave system. The system acts like a cloak around the kennel and makes us invisible. P's one of those very snobby sorts of inventors; he told me it's called a 'Controlled Light-wave Oscillating Assimilator (Type K)' whatever that means! But being just a simple secret agent, I call it C.L.O.A.K. for short. It's so much easier to remember, and what's even better Humph, is when I call it C.L.O.A.K. it makes P really annoyed.

"Just you wait and see Humphrey. Tomorrow, aside from the news of the Queen's disappearance, the TV, newspapers and radio stations will be filled with stories of the strange noises heard above Central London. There will be rumours running around about invisible flying saucers and alien spacecraft. The funny thing Humph, old man, is the aliens are just you and me!"

"*Geronimo!* yelled James, then pulled hard back on the control stick, sending the kennel speeding in the direction of the MI6 building. Humphrey looked over at the wall screens. James was right. Little groups of people and animals stood together, looking skywards, trying to make out where the noise was coming from. From the blank expressions on their faces, it was clear to Humphrey that they couldn't see a thing and did not have a clue what was happening.

In a few minutes, the kennel was hurtling along at 300kph just a few feet above the grey waters of the River Thames.

"There it is!" cried James.

Up ahead was the impressive outline of the famous MI6 building. Everyone who knew about the MI6 building thought it was a thrilling place, as it was known as the home of the British Secret Service and training ground for the country's top-secret agents. It was also home to some of the best scientists and engineers in the world. They worked deep beneath the building in top-secret bunkers, creating, testing and building some of the most advanced and effective gadgets in the planet. Only a few carefully-chosen animals knew that the building was also the secret home of CI6 (Canine Intelligence 6), a top-secret base for James Bone 007 and all the other CI6 secret agents.

Instead of heading towards the front entrance of the building, James flew the kennel round the back and hovered over the car park. A message flashed up on the kennel's screens: 'Clear to land in space number 10'. James carefully maneuvered the kennel to hover just above the right space, then landed it with a huge bump. James was a great pilot, but he had never quite got the hang of landing. As soon as the kennel touched down, the car park space started to descend into the earth, just like the deck of an aircraft carrier. Within a few seconds, the daylight above them had disappeared to a small oblong of light. Deep beneath the MI6 building, they jolted to a halt. James and Humphrey undid their safety straps, opened the kennel door and stepped out into a softly-lit tunnel. For a moment or two they both blinked as they adjusted their eyes to the dimmer level of lighting. When their eyes had adjusted, the first thing they managed to make out in the gloom was a miniature electric train.

"Quick, jump on the train Humphrey, it's for us. We have to check-in with C as quickly as possible."

"Who exactly is this C?" Humphrey asked, jumping

into an empty seat.

"Well now, you will just have to wait and C, if you 'C' what I mean!" laughed James, as he settled in the seat next to him.

The train journey was very quick; so quick that it seemed like it was over before it began. "We've arrived," announced James, leaping athletically out of the train and onto the platform. Humphrey followed closely behind him.

"What's next James?" Humphrey asked excitedly.

"We go through these rather smart glass doors into a really super express lift, which whooshes us up 21 floors to C's rooftop office," said James.

The lift doors closed silently behind them. After a slight pause, the lift accelerated at such a rate that it made their ears pop. Slowing down rapidly as they approached the 21st floor, the lift came to a halt and the doors silently slid open.

"Over there!" yelled James, stepping out of the lift and rushing across the huge flat roof towards a small brick building, standing at the far corner. James got there first and paused for a second or two to catch his breath. He then pressed his paw against a small, silver screen mounted in the wall. The screen sensor recognised his paw-print and immediately lit up. Slowly, the heavy, metal door began to open.

"Okay, follow me," said James, walking confidently in through the open door.

Suddenly, a huge Irish wolfhound stepped forward and blocked his progress.

"Hello there! And a warm welcome back to you, Mr Bone," said the hound in a soft Irish accent. "Your friend there must be Humphrey, the Downing Street cat, if I'm correct? I have to say, your photograph doesn't really do you justice, Mr Humphrey. By the way, I'm Shamus 'O' Farrell, one of C's team of bodyguards. Gentlemen, if you would be good enough to follow me, C is in the boardroom awaiting your arrival."

"Don't think I'd like to bump into him on a dark night," whispered Humphrey to James, as they followed the huge shadow of Shamus down the corridor and into the boardroom.

C was standing at the far end of the room, casually looking out of the window. She heard them enter and very slowly she turned around. Humphrey was instantly struck by her appearance. She was a very tall, very slim cat, with a lusciously long, black, shiny coat. An impressive streak of white fur ran from between her eyes, over her forehead, and all the way down her back to the tip of her long, elegant tail. Effortlessly, she glided across the room to greet them.

"Hello James, I've been expecting you," Her voice was smooth, mellow and slightly husky. There was a trace of an accent in her voice, which Humphrey could not quite place. He thought that it was possibly Middle Eastern, maybe Turkish or Egyptian.

"This of course, if I am not mistaken, is your very good friend Humphrey," she said as she turned to face him.

"Well, I've seen you on television with the PM so many times, Humphrey, I feel like I know you well." She fixed her eyes on his directly, and he was hypnotised by the brightest pair of ice blue eyes he had ever seen. Her intense gaze quite unnerved Humphrey and he stumbled over his reply.

"I, er ... I must say, you're not exactly what I was expecting, C, but it really is a pleasure to meet you," he replied.

"Well, I'm not surprised I'm not what you expected, Humphrey," she laughed.

"Everyone meeting me for the first time automatically expects the Head of Canine Intelligence to be male and *canine*, not female *and feline*. But CI6 is an equal opportunities employer," she laughed. "So, all types of animals get an equal chance to rise to the top here. Anyway, why should dogs and boys have all the best jobs... and get all the best gadgets to play with?" she said, with a playful wink. Then she linked arms with both of them and led them into the boardroom.

When they were all comfortably seated her tone

changed and she asked them firmly, "Well, boys, tell me, how are we going to find the Queen and, more importantly, when we have found her, how are we going to rescue her?" Those ice-cold blue eyes darted from one to the other as she waited for an answer.

James, not in the least bit phased by C, spoke first. "I plan to visit the palace immediately, C. I shall speak with the corgis, the palace cats and any of the other animals to find out if they have any information to offer. After that, it's off up to Baker Street to see my old pals, Holmes and Watson.

Everyone reckons Holmes is getting a bit past it, but I believe he's still the best bloodhound in the business. As for Watson, his research methods are the most thorough and modern I've ever come across, and that includes P and all those snobby boffins here at CI6."

"Very good, James, that's really most impressive. I fully approve of your plans," said C, smiling. "But you must try to be kinder to dear old P. I know you two don't get along, but that's mainly because you keep breaking all the gadgets he designs for you, James. Now what about you Humphrey, have you any good ideas you want us to hear?"

Humphrey was quite surprised to be asked his opinion; after all, he wasn't a secret agent, he was just a humble cat who happened to live next door to the Prime Minister of Great Britain. He thought as fast as he could, desperately wanting to impress C by coming up with an idea as impressive as James', but his mind was simply a blank. Just as he was about to give up, an idea sprung into his mind. "I've got it!" he shouted, as he got up from his chair.

"Technology has to be the answer to solving our problems. Let's get the CCTV tape recordings from all the cameras that are mounted in and around the palace and examine them. They may just give us a clue as to where we should begin our investigation."

"That's splendid, Humphrey, absolutely splendid. Leave that task with me, while you go and help James up at the palace. I'll get the team from the technical department to sort out the CCTV tapes immediately."

C smiled at them as she reached across the table for the phone. James and Humphrey missed her smile completely; they were far too busy trying to keep up with Shamus 'O' Farrell, who was leading them back to the flying kennel at a furious pace.

CHAPTER FOUR - A VISIT TO BUCKINGHAM PALACE

"Hello, I am most sorry to interrupt you... it's Winston here again. I do hope you are enjoying the story so far. I must say, I am so pleased I decided to start writing this story. My memory bank is whirring like a computer, and I can remember the dreadful day when our dear Queen was kidnapped like it was yesterday. Well, right I'm off, so 'toodle pip' to you all. I must get back to my desk and finish writing the story while the thoughts are still fresh in my mind."

No sooner had Humphrey's bottom touched his

seat than the platform started to rise up towards the daylight and the roof of the CI6 building. James was in a big hurry and did not wait for the car park space to lock back into place; he began firing up his engines when they were only halfway back to the surface. The kennel roared off the car, park roof and briefly hovered overhead while they prepared themselves for their journey.

"Strap in, Humphrey or I will be scraping you off the floor," laughed James, as Humphrey fumbled with his safety belt. James switched on the C.L.O.A.K. system, then paused to give Humphrey a chance to finish belting up. As soon as Humphrey was ready, James hit the lever and the kennel whizzed across the river. James made a tiny steering adjustment towards the left, then gunned the kennel straight down the Vauxhall Road towards Buckingham Palace. As they hovered above the palace gardens, James threw a glance in Humphrey's direction. The poor old thing looked like he was ready to throw up.

"Sorry about that, old boy, bit heavy on the throttle I'm afraid. I'll try to be a little more careful next time." As usual, James landed the kennel with a huge bump, causing Humphrey to turn a whiter shade of pale.

With his head spinning and his stomach churning, Humphrey slowly loosened his seat belt. For a moment he wondered if he really wanted there to be a next time.

The two friends climbed out of the kennel and quickly made their way to the kitchens, being very careful to avoid getting spotted by palace staff. As they approached the kitchens, a tubby, little corgi let out a welcome bark.

"Shush…" said James, rushing over to the corgi. "It's very good to see you Clarence, old man, but do try to keep the noise down. We are on a top-secret mission and we want to keep it that way!"

"No problem, James. The truth is, I saw you coming and I'm afraid I was so pleased to see you, I, er… got a little too excited and carried away. By the way James, I must ask, who's that odd-looking fellow you've brought with you?"

"That's Humphrey, the Downing Street cat, and he's not at all odd, Clarence. He's just feeling a little sick, probably something to do with my driving, I think," laughed James.

"Humph lives next door to the PM over in Downing Street, and right now he's helping me on this very secret mission. He's a great chap, my best friend in fact, and I'd trust him with my life. So please, be sure to help him out Clarence, and tell him anything you would tell me, old bean," said James.

"Of course, James. Any friend of yours is a friend of mine. I will help him all I can," replied Clarence.

"By the way Clarence, old boy," said James with a twinkle in his eye, "you must have been sitting under the table at a heck of lot of banquets since I last saw you." He gently poked Clarence a couple of times in his rather ample stomach.

"Yes, I'm afraid you're right, James. I badly need to get down the gym, do some 'Tums and Bums' or whatever they call it nowadays."

"That's what you told me last time we spoke if I remember correctly," answered James with a grin. "Now quickly, let's get inside before someone sees us. Clarence, can you get all the palace animals together? I need to ask them a few questions."

"Consider it done," said Clarence, waddling towards a set of stairs which would take them down to a cellar beneath the kitchens.

"Follow me, chaps," he said. "We won't be disturbed down here".

James and Humphrey formed a line behind Clarence and, silently, the three of them descended the steps down to the cellar. The cellar was dry, cool and crammed from floor to ceiling with rack upon rack of fine wines. The trio managed to find a large, clear space at the back of the cellar where they sat down to wait for the palace animals to arrive.

The first to turn up was Queenie; she was head of the royal corgis and took her job extremely seriously. Queenie would always accompany the

Queen on her royal visits; this caused her to think she was something special and very important. When she accompanied the Queen, she made sure that she wore her shiny, gold crown, her favourite red, velvet coat, elegantly trimmed with the finest ermine, and her diamond-encrusted royal collar. The other animals all thought she tried too hard to be posh and thought she was a bit of a snob.

Shuffling close behind Queenie was Hamish. He was an old, ex-army, English sheepdog who had been in charge of the downstairs animals ever since he had retired from the service. Hamish would begin each day by, very slowly and methodically, taking a register to make sure that all the 50 or so animals he was in charge of were present and correct. He would start at the palace stables, which was home to ten horses, a pair of Shetland ponies, two cows, four sheep and six West Yorkshire terriers, led by a cheeky chap called Jeff. When these had all been safely accounted for, he would move on to the animals in the outbuildings and gardens. Finally, he would account for all the animals that lived in the palace itself.

A large assortment of cats arrived next, led in by Jeff. The cats lodged in the downstairs ballroom and did a great job keeping the palace free from mice and rats. Jeff was a bit of a joker who annoyed Hamish, as he wouldn't do as Hamish told him.

Poor old Hamish. Trying to get 50 different animals to do what he wanted was a very difficult task.

Living out in the palace gardens was a large, shiny tortoise called Speedy Gonzales, along with a weird pair of flamingos who strolled across the lawns liked they owned the place. Finally, I must remember to mention Fred and Florence, a pair of very snooty peacocks. For some reason, known only to her, the Queen was very fond of Fred and Florence (or Fed and Flo as she called them). Each morning, before her breakfast, the Queen would make a point of personally visiting the gardens to feed them.

In no time at all, the entire cellar was crammed full of animals, keen to find out what was happening. James decided he would climb up on top of a wire rack to make sure everybody could see and hear him when he spoke.

"You've all probably heard the bad news by now, but for those of you who haven't, late last night Her Majesty the Queen was kidnapped from the palace. I've come down here today to find out if any of you saw or heard anything unusual last night."

For a few long moments the room was silent. It was so quiet that if you had listened carefully, I do believe you could have heard a spider walking across the cool stone floor. Suddenly, from the far side of the room, a rough-sounding London accent split the air.

"Hello guv, I'm Julius Germanicus. The, er, let me see, how would you put it? I suppose I'm what you'd call the garden cat." Standing by the open door and looking very cocky, was a great big, ginger cat. "I don't come indoors very often, guv. Hamish won't let me in. He thinks I'm a bit downmarket. In fact, this is only the second time I've been inside a palace building since I was born." He laughed roughly before continuing.

"Yeah guv, I, er, I heard sumfin last night. Saw sumfin as well actually. Fought it was a bit odd at the time, but not odd enough to make me wanna do anyfink about it, if you see what I mean."

He looked round at the other animals with his sharp, yellow eyes, waiting to see if any of them would pass a comment. The majority of the animals knew Julius Germanicus pretty well. Over the years he had developed a reputation for being argumentative, aggressive and a bit of a bully who was much too full of his own importance. Most of the palace animals disliked him intensely and made a point of keeping out of his way.

"What exactly was it that you saw… big boy?" asked James in a slightly mocking manner. He was not the least bit worried by Julius Germanicus' attitude or reputation. Over the years, James had dealt with a host of different types of bullies and ruffians from all corners of the world; one more wasn't going to throw him into a panic. Humphrey thought differently and hurriedly scrambled up besides James on top of the wine rack. He caught his breath then whispered to James to be careful how he spoke to Julius Germanicus, as he was a ginger cat and ginger cats were renowned for having very short tempers and getting into fights.

"Thanks, Humph, old boy. But don't worry, I've met his kind many times before, and in my book, brains usually beat brawn. From where I'm standing, chubby, old Julius Germanicus has plenty of brawn, but not too many brains," he chuckled.

Julius Germanicus heard James' "big boy" comment, but he pretended he hadn't and let it fly right over his head and out through the open door.

"Right you are, governor," said Julius Germanicus as he pulled himself up to his full height and puffed out his chest. He liked being the centre of attention and he was beginning to feel quite important.

"It was like this, guv. Late last night I was having a kip on a wall, the low brick wall just next to the fountain in the big courtyard. Suddenly me luverly dream was disturbed by the noise of a van pullin' up right in front of the kitchens. Soon as the 'ole van stopped, the kitchen door banged open and a butler comes out to meet the driver. It was that snotty butler. The one we all calls 'Posh Jonathan'. You all know the geezer I'm talking about." He looked around the crowded room menacingly and a few of the animals nodded their heads.

"Well, Posh Jonathan takes a couple of trays of pizzas off the driver and goes back inside. Me, I finks nuffin' more of it and goes straight back to me 40 winks. I'd hardly closed my eyes when the kitchen door bangs open again. Two geezers, both dressed in black, come out of the kitchens carrying a big bundle between them. They shove it in the back of the van then jump in the van and drive off. That was it, excitement over for the night. After that, I, er, just curled up and went straight back to kip."

"Thank you, Julius Germanicus. You have been of great service," said James.

"Who knows, if you ask Hamish nicely, he may even let you in the palace buildings more often."

"Fink nuffin' of it, guv. It's a pleasure to be of help to the fuzz. I'm presumin' you are a member of 'Er Majesty's constabulary forces?" he asked, flashing James a leery-looking grin.

"By the way, officer, if you do manage to find Her Highness, er… don't forget me when they are givin' out the rewards will you?" He laughed.

His words fell on deaf ears as James had already moved on and was asking other members of the crowd if they had seen anything worth reporting. James carefully searched the faces round the room, hoping for some response. All he got back was the low murmur of conversation as the animals talked amongst themselves.

Without warning, a bit of a fuss broke out at the back of the room. Then the crowd parted and a small animal pushed its way through until it was in standing right in front of James.

"Mr Bone, Mr Bone! I must speak with you. I saw everything Julius Germanicus saw," it said in a shrill and anxious voice. James looked down to see where the sound was coming from. Looking up at him was a tiny, brown field mouse. Without a moment's hesitation, James leapt from his perch on the wine rack and landed right beside the mouse.

"My goodness me, you're taking a big chance coming in here," he said to the mouse. "You could easily end up as someone's lunch. There must be at least a dozen or so dangerous-looking cats in the room. All I can say, is its lucky for you that they're all very well -fed."

"Yes, you're so right Mr. Bone," replied the mouse as it darted nervous glances around the room. "My heart is beating furiously and I have never been so scared in my life. But I had to tell you what I saw. It may help you rescue the Queen."

"What did you see?" James asked as he sat down besides the mouse. "Oh, and by the way, what's your name?"

"My name is Henrietta Brown and, as I said, I saw

everything Julius Germanicus saw. Except I was lucky enough to see a little more."

"Do go on, you are making me very curious," said Humphrey, who had also jumped down from on top of the wine rack to join them. Henrietta was so startled by Humphrey's sudden arrival that she ran to hide behind James.

"Don't worry, Henrietta, Humph won't hurt you, he's with me," said James.

"Oh, thank goodness for that, James. For one horrid moment, I thought I was about to become the dish of the day," said Henrietta in a very shaky voice.

"Well," she went on, "as I was saying, I saw everything and a few things Julius Germanicus missed. For a start, painted on the side of the van was the name of the pizza delivery company and I managed to remember it," she said triumphantly.

"Fantastic!" cried Humphrey.

"What was the name?" asked James.

"The name of the company was 'Don Corleone: the Original Stone-baked Pizza Company'. And I can remember the slogan that was painted under the name. It said, 'Don Corleone – he'll make you a pizza you cannot refuse'"

"That's not all," she continued excitedly. "I also saw three men, not just the two men that Julius Germanicus spoke of. They were all dressed in black and the three of them came out of the kitchens carrying a big, black sack between them. They bundled the sack into the back of the van and closed the doors. After that, two of them jumped into the van and drove off, while the other one disappeared into the palace gardens."

"Well, thank you so much for that, Henrietta, you have been an enormous help. Now we really have some information to go on. Humphrey will see you safely back to wherever you want to go, and let me say once again, we can't thank you enough for being brave and courageous enough to come into this hostile environment and tell us what you saw. That was not an easy thing to do. You have our utmost admiration, Henrietta," said James sincerely. "Now please allow us to let Jeff and his West Yorkshire terrier friends escort you back to your home. You will be perfectly safe with them.

"Quite right, nobody messes with a pack of Yorkies," laughed Humphrey.

"Thank you. I will accept your kind offer and it was my pleasure," replied Henrietta. "I am pleased to have helped and wish you both much luck in your search to find the Queen." Humphrey led Henrietta back through the crowd, past Julius Germanicus, who was still leaning idly on the door. As Henrietta passed Julius Germanicus, he flashed his sharp claws and gave her a look that made the hairs on the back of her neck stand up. She felt certain that if James and Humphrey had not been by her side, Julius Germanicus might have been enjoying a mouse sandwich for his lunch.

Humphrey and James met outside in the palace gardens to decide what to do next.

"What do you think Humph, old chap?" asked James, as they hid behind a large hedge to avoid being spotted by palace staff.

"Well, I think Henrietta is an absolute star. It takes a lot of courage for a small mouse to enter a room full of fearsome cats. In my book, she really is exceptionally brave."

"Yes, you're right, she is very brave and very observant, and she has given us some wonderful information to work with. But next I think we should fly up to Baker Street to meet with my old friends, Holmes and Watson. I would like to see what they think about the information we've gathered so far."

"Good idea James, let's get started." Humphrey was already sprinting towards the kennel. Suddenly, he slid to a stop and turned back towards James.

"Oh, by the way James, I meant to say to you, I'm not really sure about Julius Germanicus. There's something not quite right about him. I don't know what exactly, but I think we need to keep an eye on him."

"I agree Humphrey, old boy. To my mind, he tries a bit too hard to be the chirpy cockney character.

I wouldn't trust him as far as I could throw him!" shouted James, as he ran to catch up with his friend. "I have already asked a couple of the palace animals to keep an eye on him and feedback any information they gather. Now come on, let's get the kennel fired up and over to Baker Street as fast as we can."

CHAPTER FIVE - BAKER STREET

A few minutes later they were heading out over Green Park, towards Park Lane. As they passed overhead, Humphrey managed to catch a brief glimpse of the Horse Guards exercising their horses in Hyde Park. Then it was up, over Marble Arch, across Portman Square and straight on up to Baker Street.

"What number do we want?" James asked Humphrey,

as he fiddled around, programming the kennel's satnav system.

"221B Baker Street, Humphrey. And make it fast, we are almost there."

The satnav locked on and the kennel glided safely down to land with a massive bump on the roof garden of 221B Baker Street, home to the famous private investigator, Sherlock Holmes. As soon as they disembarked from the kennel, a slightly chubby, friendly-looking dog, wearing a beaten-up hat and glasses, scurried over to greet them.

"Hello there, gentlemen, my name is Watson. Dr Watson, to be precise," he said, introducing himself to Humphrey. "Do tell me, gentlemen. To what do we owe the pleasure of this unexpected visit?" he asked jovially.

"It's me, Dr Watson," said James. "Don't you recognise me?"

"Well bless my soul, bless my soul, if it isn't the one and only James Bone 007 in the flesh," stated a breathless Dr Watson.

"Do forgive my old eyes, dear boy. I didn't recognise you straight away. I probably need to make another visit to Pet Specsavers and get my eyes tested again."

"It's good to see you again, Dr Watson. We need to see Holmes and we need to see him urgently," said James, shaking Watson warmly by the paw.

Watson turned quickly and urged the friends to

follow him in through the open patio windows. Once inside, they headed downstairs to a large book-lined study. At one end of the study, wearing a well-worn deerstalker hat, stood a rather sad-looking bloodhound.

"Holmes, old man, so good to see you!" cried James, rushing across the room to greet his old friend.

"It's jolly good to see you again James, young fellow," replied Holmes in a rich, velvet voice.

James quickly introduced Humphrey, then immediately got down to explaining everything that had happened so far, not forgetting to include the information they had managed to gather from Julius Germanicus and Henrietta mouse.

"Hmm. Well, gentlemen, I must confess, you have set me a most interesting case, most interesting indeed," said Holmes as he slowly and deliberately paced up and down his very worn-out carpet.

"How exciting," thought Humphrey. "This is obviously what the great detective does when he is thinking a case through."

"As I see it," said Holmes, "on the night the Queen went missing, Julius Germanicus was the first to notice anything unusual, but he certainly wasn't anywhere near as sharp an observer as Henrietta mouse was. He saw two men carrying a bundle to the van and she saw three men carrying a bundle to the van. Could it be that he's just trying to be clever and throw us off the scent? Maybe he wants to make us look in the wrong places and waste our time? Or could he be telling the truth?" "That," said James, "is exactly why we need your help."

"Gentlemen, I need time to think. Would you be kind enough to leave me alone for an hour or so? By which time, I hope to have developed some idea of what we should be doing next".

"Time for a quick milkshake I think," said Dr Watson as he polished his glasses. He briskly led James and Humphrey back upstairs to the roof garden. Sitting in the evening sunshine, the three of them relaxed, drinking Watson's homemade raspberry milkshakes (Dr Watson cleverly remembered that James preferred his shaken, not stirred).

Down below, in his book-lined study, Holmes was carefully putting his thoughts together.

"I can't believe we have been on the go since early this morning," said Humphrey. He moved off his seat, stretched all four legs and arched his back, in one smooth, athletic movement.

"I say," said Dr Watson, "I wish I could still stretch like that. Oh, to be young again like you, Humphrey. You simply don't know how lucky you are. One day you will wake up and you won't be able to stretch that way, so you had better enjoy it while you can."

"If you think that's good, watch this," said Humphrey,

showing off by performing a perfectly-executed back-flip.

"Bless my soul, Humphrey. That shouldn't be allowed. You've just made me feel 101 years old!" exclaimed Watson with a snort.

James took the opportunity to rib his old friend. "Watson, you're starting to turn into a grumpy, old man. If you keep on like that, we will have to send you off to the Battersea Dogs Home."

"There's not a chance of that, James. I rarely travel south of the river if I can help it," he replied quickly. "Now just watch this," he commanded, jumping up from his chair. He took a few quick steps forward then flipped himself head over heels through the air and finished with a perfect landing. Somehow, he had even managed to keep his hat on.

"Bravo, Dr Watson, bravo!" yelled Humphrey. "Yes, bravo and well done!" echoed James.

Dr Watson gave a gentle nod in their direction before returning to his chair. "Still life in the old dog yet, gentlemen... I am afraid Battersea Dogs Home will have to wait a little bit longer."

The three of them had a marvellous time chatting, until Dr Watson looked at his pocket watch and suggested it was time to go back downstairs and see how Holmes was getting on. They made their way down to the study to find Holmes hidden behind a pile of books. There were books on the table, books on the floor; even the telephone had a pile of books balancing precariously on top of it.

"Goodness me Holmes, I do believe you are drowning in an ocean of books!" cried Humphrey.

"You're quite right, young man. I've spent the last hour or so paddling around the edges of this ocean, before finally deciding to dive in and do some serious fishing," replied Holmes in his deep tones.

"Tell me James," asked Holmes in a very serious tone, "How quickly can your kennel get you to Italy? The village of Corleone in Sicily to be precise? And by the way, do you happen to have a CI6 agent stationed there?"

"Sicily should not be too much of a problem, Holmes. With both engines set to their maximum boost factor, I think we could be there in about an hour and 20 minutes. My problem is, we can only carry three passengers, and that includes the pilot. And, to answer your second question, yes, we have one of our top agents stationed in Sicily; let's face it, we need to have a top agent stationed in the home of the Mafia, and her name is 'Coo Chi Gucci'.

"Why do you want us to go to Sicily, Holmes?" asked Humphrey.

"Well, gentlemen, I've been checking out the information we have gathered so far. If I'm correct, and quite honestly, I can't remember the last time I was wrong, I believe we will find Her Majesty the

Queen somewhere in Sicily, probably hidden in the Mafia village of Corleone."

Holmes flicked over the page of his Italian map to show them exactly where the village of Corleone was. Humphrey took the opportunity of a pause in the conversation to lean over and whisper to Dr. Watson that he thought Holmes sounded a little too sure of himself.

"Not at all, not at all, my dear boy," whispered Dr Watson back to him. "I've been working with Holmes for as long as I can remember and I've never known him to be wrong yet."

Holmes' deep voice interrupted their whispering. "I must ask you all to trust me completely," he said dramatically. Then suddenly he turned and walked back to the bookcase at the far end of the room. The others held their breath, waiting anxiously to see what he was going to do next. Holmes slowly lent back against the bookcase, closed his eyes then began to scratch himself against it like crazy. When had finished he let out a huge sigh and said, "I am so sorry about that, gentlemen, but I'm sure you all know what it's like when you have an itch you can't reach. There can be no waiting; it simply has to be scratched." The others looked at one another then smiled and nodded in agreement.

"Now, to continue," said Holmes. "Do you all agree that the pizza company that delivered the pizza to

Buckingham Palace was called 'Don Corleone: the Original Stone-baked Pizza Company'?"

"Agreed," replied Humphrey on behalf of everyone. "But what's that got to do with things?" he asked.

James piped up in an excited voice. "I think I know the answer, Holmes. I do believe I have managed to work it out!" he yelled.

"Then tell us, dear boy, tell us all you think you know," said Holmes.

"During your paddle through your ocean of books, did you happen to discover that the first stone-baked pizzas ever made were produced in the Sicilian village of Corleone? And did you also discover that Corleone is home to the crime organisation named 'Cosa Nostra', which is better known to us all as 'the Mafia'?"

"Well done, James, you are absolutely right. I did," replied Homes.

"And did you suspect that the bag being bundled into back of the van probably contained the Queen?"

"Right again," said Holmes with a warm, deep laugh.

"Finally… you recognised that the van had the name of Don Corleone painted on the side of it, and from there it was a simple matter for you to work out that the Queen had probably been kidnapped by the Mafia family named Corleone. And what's more, she was more than likely being held somewhere in Sicily, close to the village of Corleone?"

"By Jove you're good, James. In fact, you're very good. If ever I give up being a private detective, I think you would make a fine replacement for me."

"Thank you, Holmes," replied James. "But right now, I have to get to Sicily and try to rescue Her Majesty the Queen."

"How do you plan to do that?" asked Dr Watson.

"I'm not sure yet, Dr Watson, but Humph and I really do have to get going. I would appreciate both your help gentlemen… but there's just enough room for one more to join us."

"Count me in," said Dr Watson, quick as a flash.

"What about me?" asked Holmes, sounding a little crestfallen.

"Er… let me speak to C, Holmes, and I will get her to pick you up," answered James. "I'm pretty sure she will want to come along on this one. After all, it's not every day CI6 gets a chance to rescue the Queen, is it? By the way, if she brings the flying saucer, you're in for the ride of your life, Holmes; it's by far the fastest vehicle in our fleet."

"Tally-ho!" cried Holmes, excitedly. "I will wear my best cape and my new deerstalker hat to mark the occasion."

He turned around to find he was talking to an empty room. James, Humphrey and Dr Watson were already on board the kennel.

CHAPTER SIX - THE SICILIAN JOB

In a few minutes, James had the kennel at the top end of Baker Street, hovering over the top of the Madame Tussauds waxworks. He punched the village of Corleone into his satnav, turned his engines up to maximum power and hit the throttle. With the kennel set on a south-easterly course

towards Sicily, they sped across London like a rocket. Dr Watson was absolutely thrilled to be on board and decided that he would be their commentator for the journey.

"All of you, look out the window," he instructed. "The Post Office Tower is just below us. Oh, and that's Buckingham Palace on our right, and there's the Tower of London and Tower Bridge on our left. Any second now, we should see the Millennium Wheel, Big Ben and the Houses of Parliament," he proclaimed excitedly.

"Slow down, Dr Watson, slow down, you'll have a

heart attack at this rate," laughed Humphrey. "Just sit back, relax and enjoy the ride." James lent forward and switched on the wall screens so Dr Watson would be able to see everything in front of them.

"Bless my soul, we're going so fast, I can hardly keep my eyes focused!" he exclaimed. He was totally mesmerised by the speed they were travelling at. Before long, his eyes became heavy with the strain of concentrating on the screens. Slowly they began to close until finally Dr Watson lay slumped in his seat, his mouth wide open and the sound of contented snoring surrounding him.

It was very unusual for James to find himself flying the kennel at full blast, and it demanded his full attention. He was grateful that Humphrey was along as co-pilot. James would carefully study the radar screen, take a quick look at the fuel, speed and temperature gauges, then make a couple of quick calculations; when he had the information he needed, he would bark out a command to Humphrey. Never one to be flustered, Humphrey would respond with a very cool and casual, "Roooooger 007," before executing the command.

In what seemed like no time at all, James was informing Humphrey that there were 10 minutes to go before landing.

"Cut the boosters and throttle her back to approach speed. Oh, and by the way, thanks for all your help Humphrey," said James.

"Roooooger 007," replied Humphrey.

Dr Watson must have unconsciously sensed the cut in speed and it woke him up with a start.

"Goodness me, bless my soul, I must have closed my eyes for a second or two," said Dr Watson, rubbing his eyes awake.

"More like an hour and 20 minutes, Dr Watson," chuckled Humphrey.

"Keep your eyes on the screens, Dr Watson," instructed James. "We are about to land in a clearing about 10 miles or so outside the village of Corleone. Give me a shout when you see a set of flashing red lights; it will be a signal from Coo Chi Gucci. She's marked out a landing area for us."

"Rooooger 007," replied Dr Watson.

"Don't you start as well, Dr Watson," said James. "It's enough having Humphrey going, 'Roooooger 007' every five minutes.

"Sorry, old man," said Dr Watson with a sheepish grin. A few seconds later, he was hollering at the top of his voice.

"I can see the lights, James, I can see the lights. Look over there!" he cried, pointing to the flashing lights on the screens.

"Roooger, Dr Watson," said James, raising an eyebrow and throwing a cheeky grin in Dr Watson's direction.

He lined up the kennel carefully, and then brought it down to land with yet another massive bump.

"One day you'll get the hang of parking this thing James," said Humphrey.

As the kennel touched down, her engines slowed down, changing the noise from a roar to a soft hum. Suddenly, right next to them, a loud noise split the air.

"Whatever's that?" asked Humphrey, shouting as loud as he could to be heard above the noise.

"I suspect that's C and Holmes arriving," replied James. "Take a look out the door and I bet you will see the flying saucer I spoke about earlier."

Humphrey stuck his head out the door and sure enough the flying saucer had landed and he was just in time to watch C as she descended in a glass lift that came down from the centre of the beautiful gold-coloured saucer.

For some odd reason unknown to him, Humphrey felt himself being strangely drawn to the golden glow that surrounded the flying saucer.

"Wow, that's so weird," he said to the others. "It's almost dark here but the glow from the saucer makes it seem like the middle of the day. The whole thing looks like it's on fire. It's so beautiful. I have never seen anything like it in my life. Whatever is it made of?" he asked James.

"Sorry, I can't say, Humphrey, old chap. It's top secret I'm afraid. You see, it's made of a number of very special materials. Let's just say that the materials it's made of are rarer than a bucketful of dust from Mars. In truth, you won't find any of the materials it's made from on this planet…"

Humphrey looked quite shocked and Dr Watson was so flustered he burst out, exclaiming, "Bless my soul, a real flying saucer! Made from materials from another planet! Whatever next, James?"

"Maybe we will get to see the little green men who helped build it," suggested Humphrey with a titter.

"You're not serious, are you?" Dr Watson asked, with a surprised look on his face.

"No, Dr Watson, I'm just teasing you," replied Humphrey.

"Now, come on you two, hurry along, and forget about Martians and flying saucers. We need to meet up with C and Holmes," urged James.

James, Humphrey and Dr Watson, met C and Holmes about halfway between the kennel and the flying saucer.

"Well, James, here we are. Tell me what happens next?" asked C coolly. Everyone looked at James and waited for his answer.

"I'm afraid I can't tell you yet C," said James in an equally as cool response.

"I need to speak with Coo Chi Gucci first. I need to find out what's going on around here. From the reports I read, she really knows her way around Sicily. She will have some good contacts. Once I have spoken with her, I will be able to figure out what to do next. By the way, Holmes, old man, I would really appreciate you being there when I speak with Coo Chi Gucci, if that's okay with you?" "A pleasure, James. I am sure we would all like to hear what she has to say." "Great," replied James.

"Oh, by the way, C," said James, turning towards her, "We've landed in a very deserted area. We're about 10 miles south of the village of Corleone, which makes me think we should be pretty safe here? But I strongly suggest we keep our C.L.O.A.K. protection switched on at all times. People are bound to have heard us arrive, and you never know; a few nosey Sicilians may just decide to come out and see what all the noise was about." "That's all very well James," said C. "but I've come all this way and nothing seems to be happening. What's everyone supposed to be doing and what exactly do you want me to do?" It was becoming obvious to everyone that C was in a foul mood. It was a well-known fact in CI6 that she was much more comfortable sitting behind a desk than being out on a field mission. C was starting to get on James' nerves. He scratched at a little itch under his collar, took a deep breath, counted to 10 and then replied to her question.

"Well for starters, it might be a good idea to change into some cargo pants and a sweat top, C. I'm not all that up on fashion, but I don't think high heels and a short skirt are the right sort of kit for this type of mission," he turned and gave the others a little grin.

"Don't... push... your... luck... with me, James Bone, or I might just decide to take away your 00 status. This time tomorrow, you could find yourself stuck behind a desk, instead of flying that nice, smart kennel I gave you," she hissed at him sharply. Then she spun quickly on her heel and headed back towards the saucer.

"By the way, C, don't forget to switch on C.L.O.A.K.!" James called after her. She tossed her head as the lift transported her back up into the heart of the beautiful golden craft. Seconds later C.L.O.A.K. was switched on and the saucer disappeared from sight.

Coo Chi Gucci had arrived and joined James and the others at the kennel to discuss what to do next. She was everything you would expect from an Italian secret agent: stylish, slim and athletic, with a very distinctive black and white coat, and she always wore black sunglasses, even in the dark.

"'Scuzzi me, James darling, but I just 'av to say, this is a now very dangerousa mission. Because I 'ava discovered that your Queen, she is being helda by the 'Family'."

"What family is that exactly?" asked Dr Watson with a puzzled look on his face.

"The Family, I suspect," replied Holmes. "The Mafia. The Cosa Nostra, of course. The oldest, most feared criminal organisation in the world, that's who I think she means, Dr Watson. And I must tell you all, if she's right and it is, as we suspect, the Mafia, then this really is..." he paused and looked at them all gravely, 'a very dangerous mission'.

"Oh, I see what you mean Holmes, old man, that family. Well, it looks like we've got our work cut out. I mean, after all, this is their territory, their back yard, if you see what I mean?"

"You're absolutely right, Dr Watson. It's sort of England versus Italy, and we are the ones playing away from home," offered Humphrey.

"Yes, that is correcta," added Coo Chi Gucci. "Ana as you say in England, all de cards they is stacked ina their favour. Capiche? Got it, guys?"

"I certainly do capiche," replied Holmes.

"But tell me this, Coo Chi Gucci. Have you any idea where the 'Family' are hiding our monarch?"

"I can tell you, Holmes. Actually, I cannota tell you exactly where they are hiding your Majesty. But since James darling contacted me, witha the news that the Queen of England was probably being helda in Corleone, I have hada my top girls on the case. They av been searching the town, high and low. Lasta night my two best agents, Dolchie and Crabbana, called me to say they hada located your Majesty and believe that she is being helda by Don Corleone, in old deserted olive oil factory, right ona the edge of town."

"Impressive work, Coo Chi Gucci. Very impressive indeed," said James, leaning back in his chair.

"James darling, I thinka you should have team like mine in England. They are handa trained, by me. They are the best agents in the whole of Europe and that includes you, mista hot shot James Bone 007," she said, with a tinkling laugh.

"Well, who knows, Coo Chi Gucci, if this mission goes well, we might just invite you over to train up all our agents."

"It would be a pleasure. Buta… James darling, what about the terrible food in England, whatever could I eat?" she purred.

Suddenly the door of the kennel flew open and in walked C. She was wearing a very tight-fitting sweat top, a pair of cargo pants, trainers and a very cool pair of wraparound sunglasses.

"Wow, look at you!" shouted Humphrey. "What happened to the city girl look?" he asked.

C completely ignored him.

"It's time for action. It's time to get this show on the road and it's time for me to hear what you plan to do, James," she announced. "I've been listening in on your conversation and there doesn't seem to be much happening around here, except of course for a lot of silly talking, flirting and joking around. I want to see some action from my agents and I want to see it now! James, Coo Chi Gucci, both of you report to me in 15 minutes with a full breakdown of how you plan to rescue the Queen. I'll be waiting in the saucer."

C was gone as quickly as she'd arrived.

"I say James, old man, she seems to be awfully mad at you," said Dr Watson, looking concerned.

"Don't worry, Watson, it's not unusual," said James angrily. "She's always very bossy, a bit of a control freak, if you ask me. She likes to think she's in control of everything and everyone, especially me. But no one controls me, Watson – especially not a cat... Not that I don't like cats," James quickly remarked, realising his comment might upset his best friend, Humphrey. "After all, Humphrey's my best friend, he's a cat and I like cats a lot. I just don't like being told what to do by a cat that hardly ever leaves the comfort or safety of its own office," said James, raising his voice, to make sure that if C was listening still then she would be sure to hear him.

Back in the saucer, C listened to James' voice and smiled at her secretary.

"Thank you for that piece of advice, Miss Sonypennie; you certainly know how to get James fired up. He seems really mad with me," she said, laughing out loud.

"I promise you, C, he's so mad, in the next few minutes he'll burst through the door with a great plan to rescue the Queen. He's such a typical dog… he likes to think he's in charge, but he's not. Dogs, they're all the same – so predictable, just throw a stick and they'll chase it. You'd never get a cat doing that. Poor old James," said Miss Sonypennie, wiping away tears of laughter from her eyes.

Miss Sonypennie's idea had certainly stung James and Coo Chi Gucci into action. Fifteen minutes after C's impromptu visit, they were in the flying saucer, standing in front of her, detailing their plan to rescue the Queen.

Half an hour later, C turned to James and complimented him. "A really excellent plan, James. I am confident the mission is in safe hands. Miss Sonypennie and I have to return to London to brief the PM, but do be assured, I will be monitoring your progress from headquarters. Good luck to you both." She turned her head away from him and winked at Miss Sonypennie.

As the saucer took off, James and the others stood together watching.

"Let's hope she'll be in a better mood when she gets back to her office," said James.

"Possibly," replied Holmes. "But I'm really not sure how I'm going to get back to London now the saucer's gone," he said in a moody grumble.

"Don't worry about that, old boy," James said as he gave Holmes a gentle slap on the back. "We'll soon sort something out for you. Now let's get this show on the road. Coo Chi Gucci, roll out the plans of the olive oil factory so we can tell everyone how we plan to break in and rescue Her Majesty!"

CHAPTER SEVEN - THE BATTLE OF CORLEONE

Coo Chi Gucci spent about an hour going over the plans and explaining the history and geography of the factory. It had once been a very large, very busy business with over 200 workers pressing, bottling, packing, selling and dispatching olive oil to the four corners of the world. Luigi Tagliatelli, a ruthless mafia boss and head of the Tagliatelli family, had been the owner of the factory. Luigi Tagliatelli had also been a very close friend of Don Corleone, the head of another famous mafia family. One sleepy Sunday lunchtime, many years ago, in Don Corleone's restaurant in the centre of Corleone town, Luigi Tagliatelli and Don Corleone had had a massive row. The two men had raged and argued at each other all afternoon. Finally, as the sun was starting to drop behind the rooftops, the row came to an abrupt and sudden end, when Luigi called Don Corleone a "useless Sicilian pig" and struck him to the ground. The crowd quickly joined in and separated the two men. Luigi left the restaurant, vowing never to speak to Don Corleone again.

The following day, Don Corleone drove over to the olive oil factory to give Luigi a chance to make a public apology. Luigi refused to even see Don Corleone and ordered his workers to throw Don Corleone and his driver out of the factory. Don Corleone and his driver were lucky to escape with their lives when a crowd of hostile workers chased them from the factory grounds.

A few weeks later, Don Corleone and a heavily-armed band of men arrived at the olive oil factory. Just as Luigi Tagliatelli and his workers were sitting down to eat their lunch in the staff canteen, Don Corleone and his men stormed the canteen and the 200 workers were bound and gagged and sat on the canteen floor. They then watched as Luigi Tagliatelli was handcuffed and blindfolded before being marched out of the factory, loaded onto the back of a lorry and driven high into the sun-scorched Sicilian hills.

If you ask any of the villagers of Corleone what happened on that terrible day, first they carefully look around to make sure no members of the Corleone family are around, then they whisper in your ear: "When Don Corleone returned back to the village later that day, he was alone. At the time, one brave villager stepped forward and asked the Don what had happened to Luigi Tagliatelli. Don Corleone walked over to the villager and for a moment or two he stared coldly into the man's eyes, then in a sharp, rasping voice he spat out the words, "You will never see Luigi Tagliatelli! He is... sleeping with the fishes.""

Ever since that day, the olive oil factory has stood empty.

"Well, that really is quite a story," said Humphrey, letting out a heavy sigh.

"Poor old Luigi, Don Corleone must be a very nasty piece of work. I think it's high time he was brought to justice," said Holmes.

"Si, I agree with whata you say Dr Holmes," replied Coo Chi Gucci.

"Thank you my dear, but I'm just plain Mr. Holmes. It's Watson who's the Doctor. Though it really doesn't matter, we've worked together for so long now, we are not sure who's Holmes and who's Watson any more. It's almost like we've become one."

"Okay," said James interrupting, "it's time to stop talking and get things moving. This is what we are going to do. Oh, by the way, Coo Chi Gucci, is the Mole on its way here?"

Coo chi Gucci answered James' question as only an Italian agent could.

"Yesa James, darling, its due to arrive in about 10 minutes. But pleasa be patient, as that means 10 Italiano minutes, not 10 English minutes, if you know what I meana." She smiled.

"Good! That's fine, Coo Chi Gucci, just enough time to explain my plan to you all," said James. As James finished explaining his plans to them, the ground around the kennel started to vibrate. It started gently at first, and then became stronger and louder, until finally the air was filled with the unbearable sound of something grinding its way through the ground outside.

"Whatever is that awful noise?" asked Hum- phrey.

"That," said James, "should be the Mole. Let's go outside and say hello."

The five of them made a strange and slightly amusing picture as they stood together, waiting to catch a glimpse of the Mole. Suddenly, with a terrific whoosh, just 40 metres in front of them, the ground exploded upwards and a huge, twisting metal corkscrew crawled out, levelled off and made its way towards the kennel.

"I'm off!" yelled Dr Watson. He rammed his hat on top of his head and tried to barge his way past the others, in an attempt to reach the safety of the kennel.

"Slow down old man, don't panic," said James. "This is 'the Mole'. It's on our side and here to help us."

"Thank goodness for that," said Watson, slowing down to catch his breath.

Humphrey found Watson's panicky reaction so funny that he had to stuff a handkerchief in his mouth to stop himself from laughing out loud.

The Mole came to a halt just before it reached the kennel. It was an odd-looking machine. It had a long, metal corkscrew nose, which was used for drilling tunnels through the ground. Behind the corkscrew nose was a long, tube-shaped body, and at the other end of the tube was another large corkscrew, identical to the one at the front.

"It's nearly as strange as C's flying saucer," said Humphrey as he walked the full length of the Mole. "Stand back please, Humphrey!" yelled James. "The F.F. Squad are about to disembark and you don't want to get flattened by them."

James had hardly finished speaking when a door in the middle of the Mole flew open and a ramp slid out. A few seconds later, 50 Great Danes dressed in black suits, balaclavas and goggles trotted in pairs down the ramp. Humphrey thought they were the strangest and scariest sight he had ever seen.

The first Great Dane out of the Mole was wearing a striking red beret. He barked a command and the squad immediately lined up and stood to attention.

"Very good, squaaad! Stand eaaaaa-zy!" barked out Red Beret. Then he walked over to James.

"It's good to see you again, James. Haven't spoken to you since that top-secret mission in Russia. If I remember correctly, C called it 'To Russia with Love'. She always likes to give a mission a title. What's this one called?"

"You're absolutely right, Claude. This one is called 'At your Majesty's Service'. I must compliment you, Claude; you still look extremely fit and the squad's looking tip-top and as smart as ever."

"Thank you, James. The boys and girls are always fit and ready for action, and from what you've told me, this mission is likely to have plenty of that."

"Very likely indeed, Claude. Look, you need to be aware, we could take some heavy casualties on this one," James said.

Holmes and the others had come up to join James.

"This," said James dramatically, "is Claude van Dram. We are very honoured to have him and his squad working with us. He is the leader of 'F.F.'; a special team of elite professional fighters. They are only called out to respond to the most extreme and dangerous missions around the world, so we can consider ourselves extremely lucky to have them with us today."

"What does F.F. stand for?" asked Humphrey. "Foo Fighters," replied Claude. "My squad are without doubt the best Kung Fu fighters in the world. Ever since they were newly-born puppies, they have lived and trained with Wing Fat Foo, the world's most famous and revered Kung Fu Master. He has trained them so they all have lightning-fast reflexes, the speed of a striking cobra, the agility of a cat and the courage of 10 lions. They have no equals in the world of Kung Fu fighting. My squad will fight to the death to rescue your Queen; you have my word on that."

"My goodness," whispered Dr Watson to Holmes. "Don Corleone's men won't know what's hit them."

"I do believe you're right, Watson," observed Holmes.

"It's time for us to go, Claude. By the way, can you fit Holmes and Watson in the Mole? The kennel can only carry three."

"No problem, James. If all goes well, I look forward to seeing you at the olive oil factory." Claude stuck out his paw and James shook it firmly.

"In that case Claude, I'll be seeing you very soon," said James with a smile.

James, Humphrey and Coo Chi Gucci boarded the kennel, while Claude loaded the Foo Fighters, Holmes and Watson into the Mole.

The corkscrew on the front of the Mole began to powerfully twist, then it bent down and dug into the earth. In a few seconds the strange machine had disappeared back underground.

"There they go," said Humphrey. "By my calculations they should arrive at the olive oil factory in exactly 12 minutes."

"Okay, let's go," said James. There was a load roar as the engines burst into life and the kennel slowly lifted off the ground.

"Right, now it's time for us to cause a bit of a diversion for our friends in the Mole!" shouted James above the roar of the engine. "C.L.O.A.K.

will make sure we can't be seen and hopefully our new missile protection system will stop us from getting shot down."

"Why do you say 'opefully James darling? And what exactly is thisa new system?" asked Coo Chi Gucci. "I say hopefully, because I have never used the new defence system before. To answer your second question, it's called S.H.I.E.L.D. and hopefully, that's exactly what it will do, shield us from any missile attacks or gunfire."

"That's very nice to hear. 'Opefully, you're right, James darling," replied Coo Chi Gucci with a grin. "By the way, you needa to put your windscreen vipers on, it's raining cats and mice out there."

"Er, I think you mean 'raining cats and dogs', Coo Chi Gucci," Humphrey suggested helpfully.

"'Scuzzi! My apologies, whatever you say in English, 'Umphrey old boy, isa fine with me."

Before Humphrey had a chance to respond, James yelled for them to look at the screen. They were fast approaching the olive oil factory and could just see it in the distance. Light shone through the broken windows from a large bonfire that blazed in the courtyard, making the building very easy to spot.

"That's good, they're obviously not expecting our visit, which means we should be able to catch them by surprise," said Humphrey.

"Don't speak too soon," said James. "Take a look at what's happening."

Humphrey looked back at the screen. He was just in time to catch the last flicker of light and to see the glow from the bonfire fade and disappear.

"Yes James, you're absolutely right. They have put the bonfire out, they must have heard us coming, I do believe we've been rumbled!" said Humphrey.

"Bit of a tricky approach to the factory," said James through gritted teeth, as he concentrated on manoeuvring the kennel into the correct position. "Right behind the factory is a huge cliff. It's too close for us to use automatic pilot so I will have to fly us in manually. So, no talking please. Tighten your seat belts and hold your breath. I have a feeling we are in for a very bumpy ride."

All of a sudden, as they drew close to the factory, long lines of white dots started to speed towards them, lighting up the night like thousands of flying fireflies. James realised immediately that they were machinegun bullets. Don Corleone's men could not see anything, so they were simply firing their machine guns in the general direction of the sound of the kennel's engines. Fortunately, the bullets bounced harmlessly off the S.H.I.E.L.D. protection system before reaching the kennel, and disappeared into the darkness of the night.

"Thank goodness that works," mumbled Humphrey

under his breath. James and Coo Chi Gucci said nothing, but each of them shared his relief as they wiped small beads of perspiration from their brows. James swiftly and expertly dove the kennel down low and flew it very skillfully just a few metres above the ground. They were well beneath the intense machine gun fire, which continued spraying bullets harmlessly into the air while the kennel sped straight towards the factory.

As they came closer, James shouted for them to hold tight, then he pulled the joystick back as hard as he could. The kennel immediately went into a steep vertical climb, hugging the cliff face at the back of the factory as it rose upwards.

Inside the factory, Don Corleone's kidnappers were totally confused by the roar of the engines above their heads. What made it worse was that they couldn't see what was making the noise. One or two of them were beginning to look rather nervous and scared.

When the kennel reached the top of the cliff, James pushed the stick forward and levelled it out. He cut back the speed then hovered as he manoeuvred the kennel into a safe position.

"Everyone, relax and take a deep breath. We are about to land," said James, bringing the kennel to down to rest with a bone-jarring crunch, just a few short metres from the edge of the cliff.

"If our timing is correct, any second now, we should see the Mole arriving," whispered James.

They unbuckled their belts, got out of the kennel and made their way towards the edge of the cliff. Lying flat on their stomachs, the trio crawled the last metre or so to the edge and peered over to see what was happening down below. They couldn't see a thing. The fire was out and the whole area was as black as coal. They could hear people shouting aggressively as they stumbled around in the dark, and every now and then a burst of machinegun fire filled the air.

Humphrey was the first to speak. "It sounds like a real state of confusion down there!" he shouted across to the others.

Suddenly the shouting and gunfire stopped, and for a few seconds there was silence, followed closely by a low, rumbling sound.

"That sounds like it could be Claude and the Mole arriving," said Humphrey.

"Which means it's time for me to turn on some lights so the Foo Fighters can do their thing!" replied James. "Don't forget to wear your goggles or you will all be blinded by the brightness," he warned.

James checked each of their goggles carefully, then from a bag he had slung over his shoulders, he took out what looked like a large tennis ball. He gave the ball a quick twist in the middle then threw it into the darkness.

It was a very good throw and the ball flew out across the top of the factory then burst into a huge ball of brilliant white light. The effect was just like switching on a set of very powerful floodlights.

"My goodness, it's as bright as a summer's day," exclaimed Humphrey. The three friends looked over the edge of the cliff again and could see absolutely everything that was happening down below.

Don Corleone's band of villains were lit up brightly by James' flare and were now very easy to spot. They panicked and ran in all directions as they saw the Mole twisting itself up and out of the ground. Claude cleverly added to the confusion by playing a loud soundtrack of gunfire and bombs exploding. Don Corleone's men must have felt like they were being attacked by a huge army.

As the Mole slid to a halt, the side doors opened and the Foo Fighters leapt to the ground. Working in pairs, they roamed through the factory, searching out Don Corleone's villainous men, one by one.

James, Humphrey and Coo Chi Gucci abseiled down the side of the cliff and were soon at the heart of the battle. James and Humphrey stood shoulder to shoulder, giving it their all. Humphrey's fitness and agility proved to be a great asset to James when he broke off to chase a fleeing villain across the courtyard. James was running at full pelt, but was not gaining any ground on the kidnapper. Suddenly, from out of nowhere, Humphrey zoomed past him like an express train, leapt through the air and landed with a thump right in the middle of the villain's back. The man fell to the floor, breathless and stunned. Moments later James arrived, panting for breath, just in time to sit on the kidnapper's chest to stop him from escaping.

Coo Chiu Gucci proved to be an excellent Kung Fu fighter and had soon dispatched several villains without even having to remove her sunglasses.

"Wow, look at her go," Humphrey said to James. "She's fantastic," he said.

"Well let's face it, she had a fantastic teacher," James replied with a wink, pausing briefly to dispatch a villain with a swift karate chop to the neck.

Don Corleone's men were no match for the super-fit Foo Fighters. The battle was soon over and the Foo Fighters herded the bedraggled and defeated kidnappers into the courtyard. By now, lights had been set up in the factory courtyard and this allowed James and the team to get a good look at Don Corleone's men.

James dusted down his coat, straightened his collar and then set about finding out where the kidnappers were holding the Queen. He spotted one kidnapper who was looking very sorry for himself. James decided it was time to use some shock tactics and went over to ask Coo Chi Gucci to speak with the kidnapper.

"You mean you wanna me to actually speak to a human, and actually let him know we can speaka their language?"

"Yes, that's exactly what I want you to do, Coo Chi Gucci. Trust me on this one. He'll be so frightened when he discovers you can talk that he'll tell you everything. After he's told you what he knows, who do you think's going to believe him when he says he's been talking to a cat?"

Coo Chi Gucci threw her head back and roared with laughter.

"Very smart, James darling. I always tell people you nota just pretty face."

She went over and whispered in the kidnapper's ear, saying that if he didn't tell her where the Queen was being held, then he would be put on a fishing line and dragged round the Bay of Palermo, until the fish had finished eating the last bit of him. The kidnapper nearly fainted. He couldn't believe he was hearing. A cat talking? He thought he must be going mad. Coo Chi Gucci called two of the Foo Fighters to her side and they leaned in close to his face and asked him the same question again. They made sure that he knew this would be his last chance of avoiding a fate worse than death.

The kidnapper was so afraid of the two huge Foo

Fighters that he broke down, sobbing like a baby. He fell onto his knees and begged Coo Chi Gucci for mercy. In between sobs he told her everything.

The kidnapper led them to an old store room at the back of the factory. The Foo Fighters broke down the door and at the back of the room, sitting on a pile of dusty olive sacks, was Her Majesty the Queen. She stood up and thanked them warmly for rescuing her. Then, flanked by two huge Foo Fighters, she was escorted across the courtyard to meet the rest of her rescuers. James and the others were very pleased to note that she appeared fit, well and in good spirits.

She stepped forward briskly and said, "I would like to thank you all from the bottom of my heart. I didn't think I would ever see my family again." She paused to dab away a tear running down her cheek. She looked across at the prisoners sitting on the ground, then squinted up her eyes before calling for James to come to her side.

She spoke quietly to him, but in a very animated and agitated fashion. Every now and again she stopped to point in the direction of the prisoners. James listened carefully to what she said, then strolled confidently over to the prisoners. He reached into the centre of the group and put his paw on the shoulder of a small, dark man, wearing a thick black moustache, a very dirty T-shirt and dark glasses.

"Don Corleone, I presume," said James.

"Si," answered the man, without any sign of resistance.

"Don Corleone, consider yourself under arrest for kidnapping Her Royal Highness, the Queen of Great Britain," said James Bone, with a great deal of emotion and pomp.

"Take him away, Claude, and lock him up in the Mole," instructed James. Two Foo Fighters appeared out of nowhere and carted Don Corleone off in the direction of the Mole.

"Three cheers for Her Majesty!" cried James. "Hip, Hip Hooray! Hip, Hip Hooray! Hip, Hip Hooray!"

With all Don Corleone's men accounted for, it was time for the Queen to return home. With cheers still ringing in her ears, the Queen gave her well-known royal wave, then along with James and Humphrey she stepped aboard the kennel.

As soon as her seat belt was fastened, she let out a heartfelt whoop and in her most regal voice she commanded, "Home James, and don't spare the horses!"

"Immediately, Ma'am, if not sooner," replied James. "Oh, and by the way, Ma'am, if you don't mind, I have a request to make of you. Very few humans know we can talk so can I ask if you would keep it a secret just between us?"

"Don't worry a jot, James; your secret is safe with

me. Now let's stop the chatter – boot this machine up to warp factor six and go where no kennel has gone before! Or just do whatever it is you do."

James smiled to himself and thought, "How amusing – the Queen must be a fan of Star Trek!"

Poor old Holmes and Watson had been reduced to scrounging a lift off Claude in the Mole, and Coo Chi Gucci had decided she would like to take the opportunity to spend a few days in Corleone, looking around the town and soaking up the history of the Mafia.

Back in London, the Royal household and most of the nation had turned out to greet the Queen. There was lots of cheering and hip, hip hooraying. Cameras clicked and flashed and flags flew from every available flagpole.

Once in a while, I like to take a look back at those pictures. If I study them very carefully, I can just make out the animals of the royal household. They are all standing together in a small group at the back of the pictures. There's Hamish, Queenie, Fred and Flo, Speedy Gonzales, Jeff and the lovely Henrietta Brown. They had all played an important part in helping to get Her Majesty back and they wanted to share in the celebrations.

CHAPTER EIGHT - UNFINISHED BUSINESS

James and Humphrey landed the kennel safely back on Duck Island. With a massive bump, of course.
"Well, mission complete, James," said Humphrey, as he was about to make his way back to No. 10.
"Not quite," replied James. "There's one more villain we have to deal with. Would you like to tag along?" he asked.

"Try and stop me," laughed Humphrey.

"Okay. Go home and get some sleep, then come back about ten o'clock tonight and I will fill you in on what we have to do," James told Humphrey.

"I can't wait James, see you later," answered Humphrey, excitedly closing the kennel door behind him.

James switched on his wall of plasma screens and watched Humphrey as he walked along the secret path that would lead him off Duck Island. Before Humphrey reached the end of the secret path, James was snoring loudly.

At precisely 10 minutes to ten o'clock, Humphrey set off from Downing Street and made the return journey to Duck Island. He and James agreed that they felt fresh, revived and ready for the night ahead.

"We are we going back to the palace, Humphrey, old man," said James. "We have some unfinished business with a certain cat called Julius Germanicus. I have had him watched by Hamish and the others and they tell me he's been acting very nervously since the Queen returned home."

James landed the kennel in the palace gardens, then he and Humphrey set about searching the grounds for Julius Germanicus. They crept around the gardens for over an hour, but still couldn't find him. Humphrey spotted a large rock and jumped up onto it, to get a better view. Well, I'm sure you can

imagine his surprise when the rock started to move. He was standing on the back of Speedy Gonzalez!

"Sorry Speedy," said Humphrey when he realised what he had done.

"Don't worry Humphrey, I didn't feel a thing," said Speedy in his deep, slow voice.

Humphrey explained to Speedy what he and James were doing.

"Well, it's your lucky day Humphrey," said Speedy. "I think you will find Julius Germanicus sleeping next to the aviary. He knows the birds get frightened when he sleeps near them, so he likes to do it on purpose. He's a bit of bully like that."

"You're dead right, Speedy. He is a bully. But thanks to your sharp eyes, his bullying days may soon be over."

Humphrey spoke into the microphone on his wristwatch and told James where Julius Germanicus was sleeping. Together they crept up on him; Humphrey from the front and James from behind. As they came in sight, James whispered into his wristwatch, telling Humphrey to be ready to go on the count of "three, two, one, go".

"Rooooger 007," replied Humphrey. "Okay! Three, two, one… go!" said James.

On the word 'go', Humphrey jumped up and down, screeching as loud as he possibly could. Poor old Julius Germanicus was frightened awake. He jumped up from his sleep to see what was happening and just as he stood up, James fired a gun that sent a net soaring over the top of him. He was snared. He struggled and pushed, but the net was heavily weighted down and would not budge. Julius Germanicus was not going anywhere.

"Well Julius, it looks like you saw more than you told us on the night the Queen was kidnapped. Who was the third person bundling the Queen into the van, and how much money did your old master, Don Corleone, promise you for setting things up?"

Julius answered James, not in his chirpy cockney voice, but in a thick Sicilian accent.

"You might hava me for now, Mr Bone, Mr James Bone, but I promise you this. I will escape and when I do, I comea lookin for a you... capiche?"

"That's what you think, but I am afraid you will be going to jail for a long, long time old boy, so I am not sure I'll still be around by the time you get out. By the way, I have to say this: I'm glad you're speaking in your native tongue. Your cockney accent was simply pants."

Humphrey and James arranged for Julius Germanicus to be taken away. After that had been taken care of, they joined Hamish and the others for a celebratory party.

Miss Sonypennie had turned up at the party, along with C, Coo Chi Gucci, Holmes and Dr Watson. In fact, the whole gang was there, right down to

Henrietta Brown. And as luck would have it, Miss Sonypennie just happened to have a long, cool milkshake waiting on the bar to greet James.

"That looks smashing," said James. "Is it…" "Yes, James. It's shaken, not stirred," giggled Miss Sonypennie.

Well, that's the end of this particular adventure. I do hope you enjoyed it as much as I enjoyed remembering it. I am off for a walk with my master and when I get back, I am going to tell you all about the time James and Humphrey faced certain death on the Orient Express."

Index

7	Dedication
9	INTRODUCTION
11	CHAPTER ONE - A PERFECT DAY
16	CHAPTER TWO - DUCK ISLAND
21	CHAPTER THREE - CI6
30	CHAPTER FOUR - A VISIT TO BUCKINGHAM PALACE
44	CHAPTER FIVE - BAKER STREET
53	CHAPTER SIX - THE SICILIAN JOB
66	CHAPTER SEVEN - THE BATTLE OF CORLEONE
84	CHAPTER EIGHT - UNFINISHED BUSINESS